TELL ME
I CAN'T

No one can save their town.
Just don't tell her that.

JEN DU PLESSIS

BEYOND
PUBLISHING

Quantity sales special discounts are available on quantity purchases by corporations, associations, and others. For details, contact the publisher at the address above.

Orders by U.S. trade bookstores and wholesalers.
Email info@ BeyondPublishing.net

The Beyond Publishing Speakers Bureau can bring authors to your live event. For more information or to book an event contact the Beyond Publishing Speakers Bureau speak@BeyondPublishing.net

The Author can be reached directly at BeyondPublishing.net

Creative contribution by Dana Bree.
Cover Design - Low & Joe Creative, Brea, CA 92821
Illustrations - Marty Dundics
Book Layout - DBree, StoneBear Design

Manufactured and printed in the United States of America distributed globally by BeyondPublishing.net

BEYOND
PUBLISHING

New York | Los Angeles | London | Sydney

ISBN: 978-1-63792-214-9 Hardcover
ISBN: 978-1-63792-215-6 Paperback
Library of Congress Control Number: 2021923131

PROLOGUE

I love challenges. And writing this book was a challenge. But it was important to me to share my philosophy about life and business. This light-hearted story is written for both entertainment and education. It is an opportunity for my readers to dig deeper into the undertones offered and at the same time, do a self-evaluation of what characteristics lead to their success.

Challenges trigger those demons we all possess that try to shatter our confidence or tempt us to give up when things get tough. This book is for both men and women who have the inner power to succeed but sometimes lack the tools to power through adversity. By following Anna Cartwright's journey, I'm hopeful you will discover your ability to crush the voices of naysayers and tap into that fighting spirit that leads to triumph.

For me, it is all about the words I use when faced with a challenge. "I can." "I must." "I will." I push the self-doubt away and pour my energy into believing I will be successful and no one will ever *tell me I can't*.

CONTENTS

Chapter 1

ANNA CARTWRIGHT

ANNA CARTWRIGHT

I f looks could kill, Anna would be in handcuffs getting measured for prison stripes. But her impeccable style could not sustain such a drastic change, no matter how justified. She smoothed the creases in her Alexander McQueen suit as she reined in her notorious temper. "Opal Springs, Colorado sounds like a fizzy soft drink. I've been the strategic planning advisor for major companies for the last eight years, and you want me to go to a backwater? Why not send one of the junior members? Maybe Jerry? It would be good training for him."

Emily Davis sighed. "I admit it's a stretch even for us. My first thought was, no, we can't relaunch an entire town." She peered at Anna. "But you do seem to have another gear when it comes to doing things that can't be done."

Emily glanced down at her desk, then up at Anna. "There's no contract yet, just an opportunity to research and see if we can mesh. It's a town with ordinary people. Just imagine no ego-driven, megalomaniacal CEOs to deal with. For the last eight years, you have been on a wild ride of successes. Think of it as a working vacation, an opportunity to reboot. Get a coffee, breathe, and come back in twenty minutes. Then we'll talk."

The Restore & Revolutionize Corporation (R&R) were global strategists in reimagining businesses. In the year following the big contagion, they'd became a very hot commodity with companies large and small. So many had been turned upside-down by the shutdown.

Emily Davis, the owner of R&R had at first declined when Brian Gardner contacted her. The owner of the Opal Springs Hotel in Colorado wanted to know if R&R would take on his town as a new project. But after more consideration, she changed her mind and called him back. She agreed to send someone to Opal Springs to assess the possibility of reinventing his town.

Millie, her personal assistant and alter ego, thought this was tailor made for Anna. Emily said, "Agreed, this will give her a chance to restructure and adapt her abilities. It'll also be a chance for her to relax in a gorgeous place. Anna is ripe for a burnout. This sounds like the perfect opportunity. I have noticed that it's easier for women than men when it comes to convincing a company to shift gears and take a new road, path, or highway. Why should it be any different with a town?"

"You know how Anna's mind works," chuckled Millie. "Why not add something she can't refuse, like more fame and notoriety."

"Leave it to me Millie. I know just how to get her to agree." Emily grinned.

*****

Twenty Minutes later

"Come on in, Anna. You may very well be right, this isn't beyond your abilities, it just isn't up to your abilities. For the right person, this is an incredible opportunity. No one has ever asked us to relaunch an entire town. I've never even heard of such a thing. We will be on the cover of every trade magazine in the world. Whoever I assign to this project, will have the power to turn it all around and make it even better than it was before. They'll be a star just like you." Emily added the coup de grâce to Anna's reluctance. "I should give this assignment to someone who I know wants to light up the night. And I'm sure that you've had enough successes."

Anna bristled and glared at Emily. *How dare she.* "Emily don't tell me I can't. You know I'm the best person for this job."

Emily paused and swiveled her chair to gaze out of the window. Then she gave Anna something very close to a Cheshire smile. "Well, if you really think you can do this, I told Mr. Gardner you'll show up at his hotel on Wednesday afternoon. Your flight is booked out of Newark on Wednesday morning. The details are in your inbox."

"For the record," Davis said, smiling. "I think this might be just what you need to get you out of your rut."

Anna exploded, "What rut? I'm not in a rut. Are you suggesting I'm getting stale, running out of ideas?" She shook her head and stalked out of the office, slamming the door behind her. Emily made her crazy sometimes. They were friends and worked well together, but Emily had no idea of the toll it had taken to make it this far.

Anna had always been an overachiever and had, more times than she liked to admit, run roughshod over her colleagues to get ahead. She wasn't always proud of her behavior. She saw the most successful men in the company doing it because it worked. Didn't that prove it was the way to get ahead, to make a name for herself?

Anna clicked down the hallway in her Manolo Blahnik pumps, pretty sure she'd been had. Not watching where she was going, she turned the corner and walked straight into Eric, her best friend in the company.

"Ouch, slow down, Anna. Those shoes are gorgeous but lethal." He leaned down and massaged his shin where the sharp toe point made contact. "What's going on with you?"

Anna looked ready to punch someone. "Davis wants me to go to some rinky-dink town in the middle of nowhere to bring it back to life. Why there, of all places?"

"Maybe she just thinks you're a good fit for the project. She knows you'll do a great job wherever you go," said Eric.

"I've been in the big leagues, and it feels like she is reining me in. Don't you think this is a step down in my career?" Despite her outward self-confidence, Anna had an insecure streak that could get in her way sometimes. "I mean, I know I can do it, but the point is, why should I?"

"Who are you trying to convince? Of course, you've got to do it," said Eric with a knowing grin, "unless you don't feel up to the challenge?"

"Grrr. Not you too, I knew you would take her side. Why is everyone telling me I can't this morning?" Anna reached out and punched Eric in the arm, taking out her annoyance at Emily on Eric's bicep.

Eric laughed. They had worked together for the past eight years, becoming good friends in the process.

"You're incredibly talented. You've pulled off some impossible feats with the large companies you've worked with. You have a gift, an instinct for what to do to revitalize and reinvent. It's pure magic sometimes. But you've got a temper. I know enough not to get in your way when you are forced outside your comfort zone, except for this morning," he laughed rubbing his shin again.

Anna hmphed and turned and wall
back. She felt tired and annoyed by eve
most of all, herself because he deserve
a good friend and her biggest suppor†

Anna finished up her day with ᴄ…ᵣ .
her workload to Eric. She wouldn't be back to her office or her
brand new loft in SOHO, anytime soon. She would have to ask
her neighbor to take care of her Maine Coon cat, Jazz. *Poor Jazz,*
she thought. *Mom's off on another adventure.* She was about to
drop off the map and into Opal Springs, Colorado. *Wherever the
hell that was.*

*****

Anna woke up a few minutes before her alarm sounded at
4:30am. She had a plane to catch but she paused before putting
her feet on the floor.

What she did for a living was travel to any city where she was
contracted, meet the people, develop a plan, negotiate, do battle,
make *most* of them happy, and move on. She loved the challenge
and made a lot of money doing it.

Sitting on the side of the bed, Anna sighed. Reluctantly she
admitted to herself that she was tired of constantly traveling
from place to place. And part of her was beginning to wonder
what she was missing. For the first time in her life, she started

, Am I happy? If I have to ask myself that, how do I *ut what is wrong? Maybe it's time for my own renewal.*

Anna got out of bed and went to the bathroom to wash her face and brush her hair. As she stared in the mirror, she couldn't help thinking about her constant self-evaluation. *Just look at me,* she thought. *What do I know about a small town and their needs? What if they all think I'm too big-city, too uppity? What if I fail?*

"Good grief, Anna," she said out loud. "Get over yourself."

She'd packed the night before for an extended stay because today she was moving to Colorado. Maybe not moving, but she was going to be there for a while.

*****

Her 8 am flight from Newark to Chicago connected with a direct flight to the Montrose Regional Airport, which according to the brochure was a scenic 75 miles away from Opal Springs. Probably headed for the world-famous film festival going on now, the rest of her fellow travelers were picked up by cars with Telluride hotel logos. Telluride was a major competitor for tiny Opal Springs which could make her job that much harder. Experience taught that no matter how small a project, word of success spreads rapidly but word of failure spreads even faster. As successful as she was, the fear of failure remained. She was more determined than ever to make this a success. *Opal Springs, here I come.*

*****

Montrose Regional was a tiny airport nestled in majestic mountains. There were no long covered tunnels leading from the plane to the terminal. Passengers left the dry airplane air behind as they walked down the plane's steps and were enveloped in a fresh mountain breeze gently blowing across the tarmac. Anna felt her shoulders relax and her breathing slow down. She collected her luggage and walked through the front doors of the terminal. The sound of birds chirping brought her to an abrupt stop which made the person behind collide with her. Anna was in something of a daze as she apologized profusely.

She could also smell fresh-brewed coffee. There was a sidewalk coffee cart situated in a small grassy area just outside the front door. Airplane coffee was abominable, and airport coffee not much better, but this smelled intoxicating, like fresh ground beans from Costa Rica.

She stopped to get a cup and spotted an older fellow holding a sign with her name. "You must be Ms. Cartwright," he said with a smile. "My name is Kirk. Let me take your suitcase; the car is right over here."

"Thank you, Kirk." She let him take control of her large rolling suitcase and followed behind, sipping the coffee. It was as delicious as it smelled. She rolled her shoulders and started to relax even more.

A 2019 Chevy Tahoe with an Opal Springs Hotel logo on the side door was parked a short distance away. Kirk loaded her suitcase 0nto the suitcase rack, then opened the passenger side door for her. On the drive to Opal Springs, Anna watched the scenery float past while listening to the non-stop patter from Kirk about the wonderful Opal Springs and how much she was going to love it and "most" of the town's residents and the best cup of coffee for miles around at the Hot Pot Diner on Main Street. He was a one-man advertisement all by himself. If all the coffee was as good as what she was sipping, she just might enjoy this assignment.

Anna finished her coffee and tucked the cup into the small floor mount litter bag. She could use another one, but it would have to wait.

As they reached the entrance to Opal Springs, Kirk stopped talking. He said, "Mr. Gardner wanted me to give you a quick tour of the town so you can form your own opinions before he meets you this evening."

She looked out the window as Kirk drove slowly up the main thoroughfare. Kirk was quiet. Businesses were half alive; many storefronts were closed. Only a few people wandered through the quiet streets. Anna was engulfed by an enormous sense of sadness, almost a bereavement. Opal Springs had been a cultural gem. Art and music had been the biggest draws. In July, thousands arrived for the Five-Day Outdoor Jazz Festival. In December, thousands flocked to Opal Springs Five-Day Wine & Arts Christmas Festival.

It was in the past tense. What had happened to the people? Why didn't they return? Her job was to find out why and fix it. *This might be more of a challenge than I was led to believe. Why would an annual Jazz festival pull up and leave this little town? Too small, too tired looking, better options elsewhere? If the music scene left, there must have been a reason. Maybe this town was beyond repair.* *Stop being a Debbie downer*, she thought. *Just because you don't see a solution after being in town for all of 10 minutes doesn't mean it's a lost cause.* But she couldn't help wondering, *what have I gotten myself into?*

Chapter 2

OPAL SPRINGS

Two years after the lock-down was lifted, Opal Springs was still, almost a ghost town. Before the big contagion, it was a charming small town known for its year-round Christmas spirit. Everyone loved to visit. Now it was like a cracked and dusty ornament that had lost its sparkle. Storefronts needed fresh paint and signs needed updating. The fountain in the center of town no longer worked and was now a rubbish collector. There was even a pile of creepy, scuffed up Christmas gnomes at the entrance to the park. Several of the shop owners were meeting at the coffee shop to talk about their beloved town.

"It has to be the contagion. We were doing fine until it started and then when it was over, what happened?" moaned Mandy Jackson, owner of the Sweet Things Bakery. "The last specialty order I fulfilled was a birthday cake for Billie Olsen's 8th birthday. Granted, it was in the shape of Baby Yoda, but *the force* is not with us. Other than that, it's just a donut here, a cupcake there. Who can pay the bills with that kind of business?"

Sue Johnson nodded her head. She was the owner of the Fine Scents Candle Shoppe. "I know what you mean. I haven't seen more than a dozen new customers in the past month. Maybe I should light all the candles at once and charge admission to watch the big bonfire on main street. The smell would be heavenly: all lilac and sandalwood and rose petals. Then I wouldn't have to worry about the bills. It would just be a pile of ash that would blow away in the next windstorm."

"Don't even go there, Sue. Your mother would turn over in her grave. She started that business when you were just a wee little thing. You grew up in that store," said Freddie Lopez who owned the Cowboy Boot and Belt Emporium. "Look at me, my shop is full of exotic hand-tooled cowboy boots and handsome leather belts with no one to try them on. Everything is collecting dust."

"I, for one, am getting tired of the town board spouting useless platitudes of 'Just wait a little longer. The people will return. You will be fine,' said Sue. "The town board, including our dear Mayor, can take their guarantees and…I'm too much of a lady to tell you where they should shove them."

Freddy laughed. "Well said Sue, but we aren't alone. It's the same for all the businesses in town. We used to be full of smiling customers most of the year. If I am honest, though, most of the businesses were half full at the best of times before the big shutdown. But now, it's a catastrophe. I think everyone borrowed money from the local bank, including me, to see us through, thinking this would be a temporary setback. Temporary is lasting for a long time. We will all be closed down for good if something doesn't turn around in the next six months."

"My family has owned this bakery, for generations. Their blood is in the brick, mortar, and soil of this place. I won't give up without a fight. I love it here in Opal Springs," cried Mandy.

"Our town has changed; our children have left for more interesting jobs and people just don't seem to care anymore. What can we do to bring everybody back? Is it even possible?" Sue said with a shake of her head.

"Well, at least we can hear what the mayor has to say at the board meeting tonight," said Mandy, "though I'm a little sick and tired of talk, talk, talk and nothing happens."

"Amen," chorused the group in the diner, as they finished their coffee and left to open up their shops.

******

The town board meeting was held once a month on Monday nights. It was packed. Every chair in the Opal Springs Hotel conference room was occupied, and the overflow crowd was standing or leaning against the rear wall. Opal Springs wasn't large enough to have a municipal building with a space big enough to hold a meeting with more than a dozen people, so Brian Gardner offered the hotel. Grumbling and dissatisfaction permeated the air. Mayor Jared Kane stood in front of the noisy, fidgety townspeople and looked around the room. He had spent hours preparing this speech. Tonight, he and the board were ready with a plan to present to the citizens, but before he was able to say a single word, Frank Olsen, who owned the Barbecue Bonanza restaurant, spoke up.

"Mayor Kane, I don't think you get it. *We* don't think you get it," he said, waving his arm to encompass everyone in the room. There were a lot of grim-faced nods and grunts of agreement. "We cannot continue like this. I haven't paid my electric bill in three months."

"Me either," chimed in a chorus of unhappy voices.

"Are we just going to give up and die here?" Katie Wilson, who owned the Enchantments and Enigmas shop, stood up and started to cry. She was rumored to have psychic ability, and people listened to her. "I'm afraid we're in deep trouble."

The Mayor lifted his hand to calm the crowd. "Yes, I understand where you're coming from. I'm sure a lot of you feel the same way. The board and I have been exploring a lot of options. There is no simple recipe for reopening a Christmas town that has lost its appeal."

The mayor paused and took a sip of water from his bottle. He waited a moment, then he continued. "We have been in discussions with a major corporation which is considering purchasing our property and building a five star-resort right here in the center of Opal Springs. They will bring the tourists and, more important, will bring money into the town."

A loud gasp was heard from the crowd. "Are you crazy? Have you seen some of those resort towns?" grumbled Frank Olsen. Others in the group shouted aloud in protest. Everybody raised their hand at the same time.

"Ok, just a moment. Now let's talk about this for a minute. There's no reason to be so negative. No decision has been made and won't be until we all understand the benefits this could bring to the town. We must agree for this to even be considered. The board and I have thought long and hard about this. Having this company come in and build a resort will help most of us, if not all. Many of you will receive money upfront for your properties to help you recover. You will get long-term contracts to manage and profit from businesses you have run for years. You will make more money than you have ever made in this town before. We'll put Opal Springs back on the map."

One of the board members, Judith Lansing, tapped Mayor Kane on his shoulder. Then she whispered in his ear, "You've got this. Most of these people like you. You're a handsome, down-to-earth guy. You know how to listen people," *or they think you are listening,* she thought; "it's one of your skillsets. Don't forget. You've been elected Mayor in the last four elections. No one has done that in this town before."

"Thanks Judith. I'd better not get too cocky. There's always a first time for everything. Attitudes can change," Mayor Kane whispered to her out of the corner of his mouth.

He swallowed the rest of the water in the bottle and turned once again to the crowd. "Are there any questions?"

Every hand in the room shot up.

"What kind of resort? Why would I sell my business which has been in my family since 1923 to work for someone else who could fire me on a whim?" Sue Johnson stood with her arms tightly wrapped across her chest. "What kind of guarantee is that, and what kind of town would we have?"

A lot of people nodded their heads in agreement. She seemed to have touched a nerve with a lot of her friends and neighbors.

The Mayor paused to unscrew his second water bottle before continuing, "The resort the company would build is known for its spa facilities and healing center as well as Broadway shows and entertainment, among other things. All I ask is you think about the possibilities and sleep on it. Come back to me with your thoughts. We will consider every idea. We can reconvene here in a couple of days. Are we all in agreement?"

Most of the townspeople raised their hands.

That's a relief, Mayor Kane thought. As for those who didn't raise your hands, I won't need your votes anyway. I don't really care what you think, as long as my stake in the game goes unnoticed until it is a done deal.

Chapter 3

FIRST CONTACT

FIRST CONTACT

After Anna's tour, Kirk pulled into the front turn-around for the Opal Springs Hotel. The building was stunning. It was a blend of western rustic and modern materials. It was constructed of wide cedar planks and columns of natural stone surrounding two-story panels of smoked glass in the front. The tall glass windows reflected the moving clouds, giving the hotel an impression of weightlessness. Vertical columns of stone and wood lifted her eyes skyward. The massive front door of cedar with rustic iron hinges reminded her of a high-end European ski lodge. Unlike the rest of the town, this establishment appeared to be well cared for, and better yet, there was nothing cute in sight.

"Welcome to the Opal Springs Hotel," Kirk said as he jumped out and opened the car door for her. He retrieved her suitcase and escorted her into the empty lobby. "Mr. Gardner said to get you settled first. He will meet you for dinner later when you've had a chance to recover from your trip."

"Thank you, Kirk; I appreciate it." Anna reached into her purse to tip him, but he stepped away with his hands up.

"No need. It was my pleasure. It's my job." He smiled, turned, and left.

That was sweet of him, thought Anna. It wasn't often she met people who didn't have their hand out for something or other.

After checking in at the front desk, she was shown to her room, which she was pleased to see, was a suite. The main wall was a wide expansive window looking out on snow-capped mountains that framed the town. The color scheme was sophisticated in aqua, cream and chocolate brown. There was a lounge chair and table by the window and a small work desk with internet connectors ready for her laptop. There was also a kitchenette. A couple of oversize black and white photos of mountains and waterfalls adorned the wall above the desk. One door led into a medium-size bedroom with a king-size bed facing the large window looking out on the mountains. The bathroom was white tile, spa-like, with a soaking tub and separate shower.

This is perfect for an extended stay, Anna thought. *I like being seduced with amenities.* She laughed and peeled off her traveling clothes and dressed in her incognito uniform of running shoes, jeans, t-shirt, and oversized cream-colored sweater. She pulled her dark red hair into a ponytail, grabbed her bag, and left the room. She was eager to get out for some exercise, walk the streets, and develop a feel for the town. She wanted to talk to the people before they knew who she was.

*****

Anna spent an hour walking up and down the streets, looking into shop windows, getting an overall picture of the state of this little town. Everything was kind of "cute" with curlicue moldings and gnomes, or maybe they were actually Christmas elves holding letterboxes, but everything was dusty and tired looking. She was never a fan of "cute," but she supposed a Christmas town had to have a certain amount of kitsch to be successful. The thought made her cringe. *Why am I here? This is such a bad fit. I don't even like Christmas. This is all Emily's fault. I never turned around a whole town, just companies. But nobody can tell me I can't and I won't go back a failure. I refuse to prove Emily right when she expressed doubt about me handling this job. Why did she have to say that? Anna girl, you have a lot to prove, now, make it work.*

As she wandered up and down the streets, no sudden inspirations came to mind. In the past, this was how she was able to reinvent the companies she worked with. She would spend a little time with the CEO, talk to a couple of employees, and bam. Almost like a sixth sense, the eureka factor would hit her, and she would know what was needed. Problem solved. It didn't happen overnight, she still needed to submit papers and financial sheets and projections, but she knew what she was doing. It was just wrapping up the details.

Opal Springs was outside her safe zone. *I guess that was the idea,* she thought. Emily Davis wasn't CEO of R&R for no reason. She had an instinct for what projects fit best with which members of her team. Anna would just have to trust her. She really hoped her last quip to Emily, *don't tell me I can't,* wouldn't come back to bite her in the butt.

She would get a better idea if she could talk to some of the people living here, but right now, she smelled coffee. The delicious aroma of fresh-ground coffee. *What is it? The air out here?* She thought. *The coffee can't be that good.* Looking across the street, she spied Kirk's beloved Hot Pot Diner for the best coffee in town. Might as well give it a try.

Walking up the steps to the diner, she stopped and looked skyward when she heard the screech of something above her. Looking up into the crystal blue sky, she saw a huge eagle circling overhead. A chill ran down her spine like this was some sort of omen from this small town hidden in the western San Juan Mountains.

"Ouch, what the hell? That's hot!" Black coffee splashed the front of her sweater and dripped down her jeans as the diner door slammed into her. A tan, muscular arm reached out and grabbed her by the wrist, keeping her from tumbling backward off the steps. "Oh, oh. It stings." Anna pulled her drenched sweater away from her chest to stop the burning.

"Oh, I am so sorry, I didn't even see you standing there. Are you alright?" He released her wrist and began to mop the spilled coffee off her chest with his napkin. He stopped, "So sorry, I was just trying to clean up the spill. I didn't mean to…" he looked at his hand holding the napkin to her chest.

Anna's outrage was tempered by the look on his face. She was amused by her effect on men and took great pleasure in unhinging their cool, superior attitudes. Seizing the moment, she tossed her fiery red hair in a gesture of defiance and flashed silvery-blue eyes blazing with anger. She wanted him to feel she was ready to explode.

"You idiot, you should watch where you're going. My sweater is ruined. I could have been burned."

"I'll drive you to the town medic to make sure you are all right."

Anna was furious. The initial splash was hot, but she didn't think she was injured. "No thanks, I'll live," she snapped.

"But your sweater. I know a cleaner who is great at removing coffee stains." The stranger's rich baritone voice was full of remorse.

"Are you in the habit of dousing strange women with hot coffee so much that you have to keep a cleaner on standby?" She was edgy about this trip to begin with and now this. *Breathe,*

breathe, Anna. Calm yourself down. All is well. You will be fine. Today is just a day. Tomorrow is the future. She quoted one of the mantras she used to soothe her temper when it got out of hand. Her desire for coffee gone; she turned around and started to walk away.

"Wait, how can I find you to make amends. Again, I am devastated. I am not often so clumsy."

Without thinking or looking back, Anna snapped. "I am at the Opal Springs Hotel. I will leave the sweater at the front desk. I hope you can clean it. It is my favorite. It looks like it's ruined but surprise me."

Looking at her, he said, "I will take care of it." *Oh Lord*, he thought. *I have a bad feeling about this.*

Anna was in a foul mood as she walked back to the hotel. "Great start to my Opal Springs working vacation," she murmured. "So much for the eagle's omen. I thought they were supposed to bring a higher perspective, victory, and power, not a hot bath of caffeine."

By the time she reached the hotel, she had calmed down enough to think straight. Peeling off her stained and soggy sweater over the top of her damp t-shirt, she handed it to the front desk clerk. "I had an accident. Someone is supposed to be stopping by to take this to the cleaners."

"Yes, ma'am, the hotel has an excellent cleaning facility for clothes if this person doesn't show up. I can send it there if you wish."

"Thank you. I would appreciate it."

She walked up the wide stairs to the second floor and down the hallway to her room. Entering her bathroom, she turned on the hot water for the soaking tub. There were packets of Epsom salts and lavender bath oil filling a small silver leaf basket. Opening a couple, she poured the contents into the tub and watched them fizz in the hot water. After she pulled her damp t-shirt over her head, she inspected her chest to see if she was injured. There was no evidence of her encounter with the coffee. She knew she had a dinner appointment with the elusive Brian Gardner in a couple of hours so she was hoping a bath would tone her temper down, relax her tense muscles, and prepare her for the first stage of her assignment. *What do these people want from me?* It seems like somebody always wanted something from her. *What do I want from me? I don't have time for this introspection right now. I'm here to do a job and I'm going to do it, no matter what people say.*

Chapter 4
THE CRYSTAL TEARDROP

Anna dressed for her dinner with the yet-to-be-seen Brian Gardner. She didn't have a clue what he looked like. She just hoped he wasn't short, nothing against short guys, just most of them seemed to feel insecure next to her 5'7" frame, 5'10" in heels. Sometimes, she would do business with the heads of companies who exuded a Napoleonic complex. They were under 5'5" and gravitated to her height in some kind of Josephine adoration by overcompensating for their short stature. It didn't mean they weren't intelligent, just a little insecure around tall women. It was kind of funny and sad.

She pulled a short black linen jacket over a lavender silk blouse with a modest vee neck, perfectly matching a slim black linen skirt. She slipped her stocking-clad feet into her favorite Jimmy Choo deep-purple pumps. She finished her light make-up, with pale coral lipstick and deep-brown mascara. Smoothing out her mahogany hair in a sleek pageboy, she thought, *elegant but not over-the-top.* She didn't want to come on as too sophisticated. After all, this was Colorado, home of elf mailboxes, cowboy boots, and clumsy strangers. *Oh, and let's not forget the really good coffee.*

The text message said to meet him in the lobby at 7:30. After one last quick glance in the mirror to make sure there was no lipstick on her teeth, Anna left her room and walked down to the main lobby. A few people were wandering about or sipping cocktails in front of one of the enormous glass panels overlooking the mountains, but the big room still felt empty. The hotel was suffering from the lack of visitors, just like all the other businesses in town, but at least, this place was immaculate. She was looking forward to what Mr. Brian Gardner was going to say. He'd invited her out here. He must have something on his mind worth the expense.

"Ms. Cartwright." Anna turned to see the concierge holding out a large silver-paper shopping bag. "A gentleman left this for you at the front desk."

"Thank you." She was puzzled what this could be. She was not fond of surprises, too many times they turned out to be unpleasant, but that was a long time ago. Funny how her father shaped her life, was still shaping her responses to situations. He was great for promising but never delivering. She was sure it's why she learned to be so independent. At least she could thank him for something.

Anna looked at her watch, glad she had a few minutes before her dinner appointment, so she took the time to set her briefcase down on a side table and opened the bag. Inside was a package wrapped in white tissue paper with a silver bow. She pulled it out, untied the ribbon, and unfolded the paper surrounding her once coffee-stained sweater. It was clean and creamy white again, stain-free. "Oh, lovely," she murmured. On top of it was a small velvet box. She opened it and saw a glistening quartz crystal teardrop with a small deep-purple amethyst at the top, attached to a delicate silver chain along with a handwritten note.

Here is something so you will never forget the beautiful, crystal-clear Colorado air.

Anna took a deep breath; amethyst was her mother's favorite stone, a gem she wore all the time. She remembered the last time she saw her mother. She was twelve years old visiting her mother in the hospital, a small vase of lilac next to her bed. Her mother was wearing an amethyst necklace, which she refused to take off. *Don't cry, Anna,* she told herself. *What a strange day this is turning out to be. First, I get assaulted by hot coffee, then I remember dad, and now this necklace is like a sign from my mother.*

She thought about the unpleasant encounter with the dark-haired stranger at the diner. There is no way he could have known how this small gift would affect her. He surprised her after all. She smiled as she put the chain with the crystal around her neck.

Pulling out a small pocket mirror, she looked at her reflection. The necklace was perfect with her lavender blouse.

Looking across the lobby, Anna saw a very tall man with coal-black hair, facing away from her and talking to some of the staff. He was dressed in a charcoal gray suit reeking of a high-end Italian designer. From the rear, it was a perfect fit. *Maybe it was his rear that was the perfect fit.* Anna laughed to herself. And then he turned.

Her eyes widened in the third surprise of the day. *It can't be. Is this the dolt at the diner who came close to drowning me in hot coffee? Who is this guy?*

He looked up at the same time, saw her, then walked over. "Ms. Cartwright, I presume?" The deep velvet tones of his voice shot a tiny electric charge straight up from her toes.

"I am Brian Gardner, the owner of The Opal Springs Hotel." He held out his hand to her in greeting.

She was speechless for a few seconds. It was rare that she got this flustered. "I believe we have already been introduced," she said, at last. "Under a cup of hot coffee."

He looked a little mortified, then regained his composure. "It is just my luck. You got a full display of one of my less than better days."

"Let's start again, my name is Anna Cartwright, and I am here representing Restore & Revolutionize, R&R for short. Nice to meet you." She stuck out her hand for a firm shake, all business now.

"My pleasure Ms. Cartwright. Welcome to Opal Springs."

He led her into the expansive dining room. Its twenty-foot ceilings were crisscrossed with large dark beams. There were tall narrow windows on one side and at the back, a stunning glass wall looked out on a vista of soaring peaks and rugged cliffs. The setting sun tipped them with scarlet. She saw a couple of large birds circling over one of the nearer peaks. If one of those was the same eagle she saw earlier, she hoped he brought better luck this time. Anna was interested in the symbolism of presumably unexpected occurrences in life. She had read that when an eagle appears, it is giving notice that one is to be courageous and to not accept the status quo. Most important, learn how to be patient with the present until one is ready for the future. Well, the present was a wake-up call, but it didn't have to be a cup of hot coffee dumped all over her favorite sweater.

Suddenly, she realized that she had tuned out for a couple of seconds and Brian Gardner was looking at her, like she wasn't paying attention. Catching herself, she smiled at him. "Every room I have seen in your hotel seems to have a view more spectacular than the last. The mountains appear to be framed like exquisite paintings."

"It is always exhilarating," Brian said, sweeping his arm upward to encompass the panorama. "The San Juan Mountains are part of the Rocky Mountains in southwestern Colorado and northwestern New Mexico. This area is known as the Colorado Mineral Belt and was a part of the gold and silver mining industry of Colorado at the turn of the century."

A young woman wearing a white tuxedo shirt, a tiny opal stick pin and black trousers emerged from a door near the bar and walked over to them.

"Good evening, Mr. Gardner. Your table is ready."

"Thank you, Miss Rose."

He escorted Anna to one of the tables next to the massive window. There was a fresh lavender orchid in a slim vase on the table surrounded by two place settings with simple white china. The silver and the wine glasses were beautiful, expensive.

A nice combination of simple and elegant, thought Anna. *And the orchid matches my blouse. My mother must be with me. I see purple everywhere.*

After pulling out her chair to seat her, he sat down opposite. He handed her the wine and drink list. "What would you like to start? A glass of wine perhaps, or something else, Ms. Cartwright?"

*****

The meal was even better than she imagined. The kitchen was a good match to the extraordinary dining room. For a starter, she ordered a peach Caprese salad. The peaches were decorated with a mint-basil and smoked-paprika-reposado tequila sauce and fresh basil. The taste was unlike anything she'd ever eaten before. Her main course was Colorado stream trout, a buttery, oven-roasted fish served with risotto that melted in her mouth but did not leave her over satiated. Brian ordered the Elk osso buco steeped in vegetables, white wine, and broth. It smelled delicious. She couldn't say no when he asked if she would like to taste his entrée. He placed a small piece on her plate. It was a sensory overload.

Over dinner, Brian discussed the situation in Opal Springs as he saw it. He told her he'd lived here for over 10 years and watched its gradual decline, even before the big lock-down. "When I first arrived, it seemed the perfect place for my dream hotel. I trained in the hospitality industry in France and Italy and know how to cater to guests, but I wasn't interested in living and working in a large metropolitan area. Then, I found Opal Springs by chance when I came out for the Telluride Film Festival and got lost driving around. The town was fresher then, the people friendly, and there were a lot of visitors coming through. Also, it turned out I have a relative living here I didn't know about, so it was meant to be."

Anna was fascinated hearing his story, and then there was his voice and those dark green eyes. *Stay focused, Anna. Stay focused.* Did you build this hotel from scratch? What a huge undertaking." She forgot all about their earlier encounter and was soon immersed in the tale of how someone who worked in Paris and Milan could end up in this little town in the mountains.

"I thought about renovating the old Opal Springs Hotel, but it was just too damaged, even dangerous. I had it demolished. The property itself was perfect but any restoration or renovation would have been more than it was worth. I brought in an architect and told him to keep it western but sophisticated. And one year from groundbreaking to finish, the Opal Springs Hotel was reborn."

"A remarkable achievement, Mr. Gardner. I am impressed that you didn't let the difficult circumstances deter you from creating this beautiful oasis in the mountains." And she meant it. It was so unexpected in this little town, but it felt like a perfect fit within the location.

"Please call me Brian, Ms. Cartwright," he said. "I'm more comfortable not being quite so formal if we are going to work together."

"If you'll call me Anna." They clinked their wine glasses together with a light tap.

Sipping on a glass of icy cold Chardonnay, Anna re-evaluated Brian Gardner. He was not what she'd expected. He was so good-looking he gave her goosebumps, appealing in a way she hadn't felt in quite a long time. And he wasn't short. In fact, he was at least a couple of inches over six feet. He dressed with great style, and yet, he exuded a ruggedness that was beguiling. To crown it all, his passion glowed on his face as he talked about his dreams for his hotel in the backwoods of Colorado. In Anna's experience, passion went a long way to making positive changes in bad situations. She oversaw the most successful transitions in companies when the people involved were passionate and committed to a successful outcome. *When was the last time she'd felt passionate about something? Rescuing Jazz, her cat off the street, maybe? Jazz is the light of her life, but life must be more than a ragged Maine Coon cat in need of a haircut and a home.*

"Back to business," Anna said, setting down her wine glass on the table. "What do you think we or I can do for Opal Springs? Also, I am curious as to why the Mayor or Town Council or whoever oversees the town isn't here with us tonight."

Looking a bit uncomfortable, Brian started talking. "The Mayor and the town council don't know I invited you here. I disagreed vehemently with what the Mayor presented at the last town meeting. I think it will do the whole area a disservice and, in the end, destroy what makes Opal Springs unique. I don't want to go to the town meeting and disagree without an alternative option to present."

This was going to be interesting Anna thought. "What does the Mayor want to do? And why do you think it is wrong?" Anna worked best when she knew all the pros and cons and who was in charge. Often it wasn't always what it seemed. She could enhance the pros of a situation and avoid the cons, making her solutions sound more palatable than the competition's. It was a trick she learned through trial and error. Convincing people she had it all figured out whether she had or not, went a long way to swaying people over to her point of view. Without having to deal with people's doubts up-front, she was freer to work things through.

"Let's just say the Mayor has more at stake than the good of the town when it comes to reinventing it. He wants to bring in a large resort company to buy up Opal Springs and take over all of the little businesses you saw when Kirk drove you through town."

"Kirk, by the way, is a charming host. He is quite talkative and loves Opal Springs, especially the coffee. Something we have in common," Anna added. "Though I prefer mine in a cup."

Brian winced at the dig, then laughed. "That he is. He has been my unofficial right-hand man since I arrived. I couldn't have navigated the pitfalls of small-town politics without him."

For the next hour and a half, they continued discussing the myriad options Brian considered, but none of them seemed right to Anna.

"I don't want the town to sell out. I've seen this happen too many times before, and it's never good for the citizens. But I'm not sure exactly what we need," said Brian.

"The town council is holding another meeting tomorrow night to discuss the Mayor's plan. I would like you to be present but, in the background, so you can give me your honest opinion about whether to bring a large resort into Opal Springs."

"I was going to suggest that myself," said Anna. "I think I'll spend tomorrow walking around town and meeting as many business owners as I can. I want to know what they fear and what they hope for. I won't tell them why I'm in town just yet. I want to be more like a curious visitor asking questions."

"Good idea. Would you like dessert or perhaps an espresso?"

"Thank you, but no. It's been a long day. I want to go to my room and make notes about our discussion tonight before I forget the details."

"It has been a pleasure, Anna," Brian said, kissing her hand as they stood up.

"Thank you, Brian; dinner was delicious. Oh, and thank you for taking care of my sweater. I said to surprise me, never thinking for a minute it would be this big a surprise," as she looked around the dining room and then turned to face him again. She did not mention the pendant; it felt too personal to talk about. She knew he saw it and appreciated the fact that he did not say anything about it either.

Brian smiled at her and thought, *she's wearing the crystal quartz with the amethyst. After a rough start, things are getting better.*

Chapter 5

WALKABOUT

WALKABOUT

The next morning, Anna prepared for her Opal Springs walkabout. She pulled on jeans and a white button-down shirt with a mandarin collar. She used the silver ribbon from her package to tie her hair in a low hanging ponytail, put on a navy leather jacket, and laced up her black running sneakers. Odd, but she was feeling her mother's presence again, maybe because the amethyst reminded her of a devastating time in her life when she lost her anchor. She clasped the crystal teardrop necklace behind her neck and straightened it. *This little town has lost its anchor, and I will find a way to set it right. And, Mr. Gardner, what are you getting me into?* she thought. *I sense a conflict brewing here in quaint little Opal Springs. Brewing? Coffee, of course, I need coffee now.* Without another thought, she left the hotel and strolled to the Hot Pot Diner. This time she made sure to watch where she was going and managed to get up the steps and inside without another collision.

The hum of people talking, the smell of bacon and eggs, and the glorious aroma of rich coffee transported her to a time with her father before everything went to hell. They had met in a diner sounding and smelling like this one. Without wanting to, her mind drifted back to that day. He made his choices very clear, and it wasn't about her. She learned a lot from him: survival in the face of conflict, love in the face of indifference, and success in the face of obstacles. And here she was, a successful woman in a demanding business environment. Who is she kidding? All business environments are harder on women than on men, but, thanks to her father's tough love, she let nothing get in her way. She remembered very clearly the time when she told him she wanted to start her own business selling greeting cards made with dried flower petals pasted on the front. He scoffed at her and told her she was crazy; she was only 14 years old. "Don't tell me I can't," she whispered to him feeling devastated by his dismissal of her. She proceeded to do exactly what she told him she was going to do. From a card table in front of her house, she made $115 that summer selling her greeting cards to people passing. It was a lesson she never forgot.

She shook her head and snapped into the present.

"Take a seat, darling, anywhere you like." The waitress laughed in a deep, cigarette-rough voice. "We don't take reservations at the Hot Pot Diner."

Anna looked up, nodded and smiled, and chose one of the small booths next to the window, already set up with coffee cups ready to go.

"What can I get you? Coffee?" The waitress was holding the pot in her hand, ready to pour.

"Yes, please, and scrambled eggs and bacon and rye toast. Coffee first...Molly," Anna said, eyeing the name tag pinned to the waitress's blouse.

Molly filled her cup and turned to the counter to mark Anna's order on her pad.

The diner was half full of what appeared to be locals. Some were just eating and drinking, melancholy expressions flitting across their faces. Others were in deep discussions she couldn't quite make out. She started to feel guilty trying to eavesdrop but then, dismissed it. She was eavesdropping for a purpose. This was a good place to start her research. Two vociferous men seated near the rear entrance, could be heard easily.

"I don't care what he says.... I am not going to sell my business to anyone. My granddaddy started this restaurant. He would turn over in his grave to think I was even considering it." Frank Olsen, owner of the Barbecue Bonanza, was turning red in the face.

"I know what you mean, Frank, but it feels like we are between a hard place and no place at all." Freddie Lopez looked glum. "I used to sell a dozen pairs of fancy boots a week. It paid for my utilities and my taxes. Everything else was cream, but the cream has soured. What can we do?"

I want my kids to come home, but there is nothing here for them," Frank responded, not answering Freddie's question just continuing with his own thoughts. *I am stumped. This shouldn't be happening here. I've raised my kids, sent them to college, and even took vacations once a year with my wife, Sheila. I've saved some money for retirement, but not near enough.*

Anna made notes as she ate her breakfast writing down snippets of conversations. They gave her the people's frustrations and fears. A lot was going on here, and she still didn't know what Brian meant when he said the Mayor had more at stake on a personal level. She needed to do some more research.

Anna paid her bill and added a $10 tip. She'd spent some time as a waitress when she was a teenager and always appreciated a large tip. Sometimes it made the difference in being able to buy a textbook for classes or not. Or, for others on her shift, being able to buy diapers for the baby.

✶✶✶✶✶

Standing on the sidewalk in front of the diner, she looked at the town street map she'd picked up. It named businesses and places of interest. The library seemed like a logical choice to go first, and it was a just two blocks away. Librarians know everybody in town and what is going on.

The Opal Springs Library was a three-story stone building with planters filled with hydrangeas in the front. The grass hadn't been mowed in a while, which made it look soft and inviting to sit outside and read a book under the aspen trees surrounding the front lawn. In fact, several people were doing just that, immersed in books as they sat on the grass in the shade of the trees. Anna walked through the main entrance and up to the front desk.

"May I help you?" Mary Jefferson, the librarian, looked at least eighty years old, yet her dark green eyes sparkled with the energy of someone half her age. Her voice was sweet and young and made Anna want to be her friend.

Whoa, thought Anna. *This woman has a gift. I don't ever feel this way about strangers. And I bet she's a great source of information.* As usual, Anna's first instinct was to use someone to her own advantage.

"Hello there. I'm visiting from back East and want to know what to check out in this town. Also, just curious, what makes people want to live here?" said Anna.

"Thinking of moving here?" Mary asked, looking at her with curiosity.

"No," Anna answered a little too abruptly.

As if she hadn't heard her, Mary said, "Well, you started at the right place; I will give you kudos for that. There isn't much I don't know about this town. My great grandparents panned gold in these mountains, then started a general store. I grew up here and met everyone coming and going."

"I think you're right," said Anna, re-evaluating the pert little librarian. She felt an inexplicable connection to this tiny ancient woman. She wanted to know more about her, and oddly, she felt Mary Jefferson could see right through her. There would be no conning this lady, but that was the last thing she wanted. She felt like she could tell this woman anything and she would feel safe. "This is the perfect place to start. First, tell me about the library. Is there anything special here I should know about?"

"More than you can imagine, dear. Why don't you wander around a bit and then come back when you have questions."

Anna nodded her thanks and turned to start exploring. The back of the library's main room was filled with another one of those gorgeous large windows looking out on the mountains. Balconies surrounded the center of the room on three sides with stacks and stacks of books. It smelled old and mellow and safe. On the second floor overlooking the balcony was an ancient telescope attached to a table and aimed out the window. One whole section of books was about astronomy and space. Even a small children's area featured books about stars. It was charming. She spent the next hour looking at the wide variety of books available, particularly the historical selections.

A line caught her attention in one of the books on Colorado's history. First known as the Jefferson Territory, it later became the State of Colorado.

Just how old is Mary Jefferson? Anna wondered. *Could she be from the original Jeffersons of the Jefferson Territory?* Anna felt like she was entering La La Land.

At last, deciding she had spent enough time in the library, she walked downstairs to the main counter. "Thank you very much, Ms. Jefferson. Your library is beautiful. I will return when I can spend some more time here." Anna thought it unlikely that she would ever return. This was just a job.

"Of course, you will, dear. I have a sense about these things."

Anna looked at her and once again, felt this woman knew more than she was saying. Inexplicably, she missed her mother so much right at this moment that it was painful. A tear ran down her cheek and melted into her shirt collar creating a small damp spot.

"I'm so sorry," said Anna. "I don't know what's come over me. Maybe it's the jet lag."

"I know you miss her," said Mary, shocking Anna to silence. "She is here with you."

"H-h-h-ow did you know? Wait, you couldn't possibly know. Who are you?" Anna stuttered.

Mary's eyes crinkled as she handed Anna a tissue and patted her hand. "There is nothing to worry about, dear. This is all going to work out."

Anna's eyes widened, more than a little taken aback, but she smiled anyway, turned and walked out the front door feeling like someone had seen right through her, into her innermost thoughts and doubts and secrets.

Well, what an interesting start, she thought. *Focus Anna, there is a meeting tonight you must be prepared for.*

*****

Anna spent the rest of the afternoon visiting shops, taking photos of the town, and chatting with shop owners. They tried to hide their feelings of woe, but it was hard to do when they didn't know how they were going to pay their bills. Aware of this, Anna made sure to buy something at each of the places she visited.

When she felt certain she had absorbed as much as she could in a day, she headed to the hotel to change and get ready for the town meeting. Brian suggested they arrive at different times to avoid arousing suspicion. It promised to be an intense evening if what she heard from the townspeople was any indication. And Mayor Jared Kane. Who was he? And what did he stand to gain from this whole mess?

In her other assignments, Anna hadn't had to deal with hidden agendas and competing solutions. It was going to be fascinating to watch the characters at play tonight. She dressed in a black pantsuit, arranged her hair in a bun, put on red lipstick and black mascara. She chose the highest heels she packed from her suitcase. She hoped the Mayor was short. She was ready to put her reputation on the line or, at least, grab the attention of these people from Opal Springs. She felt a twinge of guilt of trying to take advantage of a situation, but only just a little. She was used to plowing through any problems that came up, because, despite her doubts, she had to project total competence.

Chapter 6

THE MEETING

THE MEETING

E very seat was filled by 7 pm. The rest of the business owners were standing in the rear of the room. The meeting was again being held in the Opal Springs Hotel conference room. Brian was standing next to the entrance, watching as people wandered in. About three dozen men and women were in the crowd, raucous and restless waiting to hear what Mayor Kane would say.

At 7:15, Anna slipped in and stood in the shadow of an alcove, just as the meeting was beginning. Mayor Kane walked onto the small, elevated stage area as if expecting a round of applause, waving and smiling at individual members of the crowd.

Isn't he precious, thought Anna? *King Kane. He looks like he's used to getting his way.* She was pleased to see he was wearing boots with one-inch heels. *Definitely insecure.* She'd met more than her share of pompous people in her line of work. It was easy to know which buttons to push.

The meeting began with questions shouted from all corners of the room. Mayor Kane held up his hand. "Stop, I can only answer one question at a time, and it won't do any of you any good to shout over your neighbors. Please respect each other tonight. We will answer as many of your queries as we can." Mayor Kane acknowledged the other three town council members sitting behind him at the table. They looked like deer in the headlights, terrified of what might happen in the next couple of hours.

Anna had to concede Mayor Kane was gifted with reasonable crowd control skills as everyone quieted down, except for the inevitable loud whispers from one side to the other.

The questions started and went on for the next two hours. Anna could tell that everyone was upset and afraid of change, but all knew something had to be done, and soon. Mayor Kane tried to soothe the nerves of the shop owners who couldn't see what this transition would mean for them and their business. A resort in Opal Springs was more than most of them could grasp. Mayor Kane showed drawings submitted by the resort corporation for the proposed transformation.

Anna didn't see many smiles in the crowd, even after they looked at the beautiful renditions of a spa. It looked like it belonged in California overlooking the ocean. Even she could see it just didn't fit with this town. She had a sneaking suspicion the drawings weren't for Opal Springs at all, maybe something the Mayor borrowed to try and get the people to agree to something not even on the drawing board yet. What advantage would that give him? Anna didn't know, but it was clear the old Opal Springs had diverged from its original path and needed something to kickstart it back into business again. The big contagion grinch, stealing their beloved Christmas town, turned it into a dusty has-been. It was time for something new and it wasn't this.

At last, Brian Gardner raised his voice over the grumblings of the crowd. "Jared, Mayor Kane?"

Anna watched Brian maneuver the Mayor, making him think he was going to get a reprieve from the unhappy residents, Mayor Kane waved his hand for Brian to continue.

Clever guy thought Anna. The mayor didn't even notice the subtle insult Brian used by calling him by his first name before using his official title of Mayor.

"Before Opal Springs, I lived in Paris, Milan and New York. Do you want to know why I could give up all the sophistication, smartness and supposed luxuries of those cosmopolitan cities in exchange for this little town in the mountains?" He looked around the room, everyone's eyes were on him. "Because there is something real about this town, there is something kind about the people who live here, and there is a sense of caring and consideration for neighbors and friends. Oh yes. And let's not forget the fresh air and the best coffee I've ever tasted."

A few chuckles erupted around the room as everyone looked at each other and nodded.

"A resort is the last thing you should bring here. It will disrupt everything in ways you," as Brian waved his hand over the gathering. "Can't imagine. And I don't mean in a good way."

Mayor Kane looked up and sputtered. "Just a moment Brian. What makes you think you are the expert here? How long have you lived here?"

Brian ignored him and continued speaking to the crowd. "I've been here for ten years now, and I consider Opal Springs my home. I've met just about all of you. I know what difficulties you have been going through, and I know you won't want to hear what problems will come in the future if you let this project go through."

"That's right, Brian, we know you. You have been a friend. You have hired some of us in your hotel in the past and offered a helping hand when we needed it," said Sue Johnson.

"What problems are you talking about?" Kirk, the hotel driver, asked.

Damn, thought Brian. *I don't want to get ahead of myself before I have any other solutions to offer. And I won't air the Mayor's conflict of interest if I don't have to, at least not yet.*

"I've been doing some research on my own. I took the liberty of inviting a corporate restoration expert to come to Opal

Springs and give us some ideas before we sign our heritage away to a resort."

As Mayor Kane started to interrupt, Brian called out. "Anna, Anna Cartwright?"

Anna was ready for the challenge, she hoped. *These are people I've already met on my walkabout. They have real fears. I may not have all of the answers,* she thought, *but I know I can do this. I just have to make them believe I can. Show time!*

Anna stepped out from the shadows and strode to the front of the room, tall and elegant, her gorgeous dark red hair and silvery-blue eyes made her standout in the down-home crowd.

There was a soft intake of breath. Many of the people already knew who she was from her visit through the town. She'd been dressed in jeans and a leather jacket and was approachable. She'd asked about their setbacks, their families, and their businesses. And she'd purchased something from every store she entered. She put her money where her mouth was which counted for a lot with these people.

Mayor Kane was speechless for a few seconds. "Just a minute, Brian. I don't recall your being a Council Member. What right did you have to do this without consulting us, consulting me?" Mayor Kane went from speechless to fuming.

"I didn't realize I needed your permission to ask for some options before this resort is a done deal." Brian was not backing down.

"We want to hear her," shouted someone in the crowd. "Let her speak."

Anna was no stranger to conflicts within companies. It was considerably different when it came to the livelihoods of an entire town. Then she fully realized the task that was before her. These people were going to need her specialized training to help them survive. She almost never doubted her abilities, but this was going to be a tough assignment. *I wonder if Emily had any idea what she sent me into*, Anna thought. *Straight into the lion's den.* Anna hoped she was as good as she thought she was.

✶✶✶✶✶

"My name is Anna Cartwright. I work for Restore & Revolutionize — R&R for short. We specialize in reinventing companies, corporations, and businesses of all kinds. You can look us up online and check out our reviews. I might even be mentioned in a couple of them." She smiled, looking around the room, catching the eye of individual people she spoke with during the last two days. They returned her smile. She made them feel special, included, like she was speaking directly to them.

"I am not going to promise you the world. Unlike Mayor Kane, I am not going to guarantee you will be richer than you have ever been."

A sudden stillness descended over the crowd. Anna had just thrown down the gauntlet. The Mayor's face went from red to white.

"What I will promise you is that I will do everything in my power to find what Opal Springs can offer the world again without selling out your birthright."

"How can you even say that?" piped up a voice from the crowd. "You've never lived here, and I'm sure you've never run a little shop in a small town. You can't do this."

"Look at the way she's dressed. That's big city if I ever saw it," said another voice, female this time.

"What do we have to lose? I think we should give her a chance. If Brian Gardner trusts her, at least we can listen to what she comes up with," said Molly from the diner.

Anna stood quietly listening to their doubts. She also had doubts but wasn't going to let that stop her from doing everything she could to help these people. "I hear you. I spoke to a lot of you yesterday and I listened. I know you are hurting, but that's what I am good at, finding solutions that can help stop the draining of your assets. If I didn't know I could do this, I wouldn't be here."

A tentative smattering of applause started then people stood and clapped until the whole room stood up and gave her a standing ovation.

Brian, standing at the rear of the room, gave her a thumbs up. "You've got them," he whispered. "They're with you." He breathed out with a deep sigh. *Now all you need to do Ms. Cartwright, is deliver the goods.*

Chapter 7

HOW HIGH
IS TOO HIGH?

HOW HIGH IS TOO HIGH?

Anna woke up early, feeling truly awful. She groaned as she tried to force herself out of bed. The clock on the nightstand was glowing 6 am in soft green lights. She had no time to get sick, too much to do. She decided a short run around the area would perk her up and clear her head. Breathless by the time she walked down the stairs to the lobby, Anna's heart was pounding, and she felt light-headed, almost nauseous. *What is going on here?* She couldn't remember the last time she'd been sick, but she was definitely unwell right now, even dizzy.

She turned around and stumbled over to the reception desk, where she saw Brian flipping through some papers.

He looked up and saw her. "Anna, are you OK?"

"I don't know. I am unsteady." Beads of perspiration dotted her forehead.

Brian came around the desk and walked over to her.

"I bet I know what it is. When was the last time you spent any time at this altitude?"

Anna looked at him. Then it dawned on her what he was saying. "Are you kidding me? Are you suggesting I have altitude sickness? How high is it here anyway?"

"8,649 feet right where you are standing. A little bit lower near the center of town."

"I've been skiing all over Europe and not once suffered from altitude sickness."

"It's in your genes whether you know it or not. If you have any one of six genes that causes altitude sickness, there is nothing you can do about it. It's so unpredictable, even if you've been hit with it once, you might never get it again. And if you've never had it, it can still knock you for a loop." Brian gave her a commiserating smile. "I've seen it dozens of times with our guests at the hotel. So far, we haven't lost anyone."

Anna groaned. "I've never heard that before. How long does it last? I have too much to do. People are depending on me." Anna stopped in her tracks, forgetting about the altitude sickness as she realized what she just said. *People are depending on me. Where did that come from?* The last time she remembered saying this was when she was talking to her mom. Her mother depended on her, and... she didn't want to think about it right now.

"You should be better by this afternoon or tomorrow at the latest. My suggestion is to take it easy, drink lots of water, and don't over-exert yourself."

"Thank you, Dr. Brian," Anna said, her voice filled with sarcasm. "Well, at least I can hit the internet and start researching options I can present to the townspeople.

Anna gingerly climbed the stairs and entered her room. She undressed in the bathroom, took a warm shower, then pulled on the fluffy guest bathrobe. As she sat in one of the soft upholstered chairs near the window looking out on the mountains, she thought, *Oh God, maybe this is a sign that I really have bitten off more than I can chew. I never get sick. I feel like an impostor. So far, I've got nothing.* Once she started thinking about signs, Mary Jefferson popped into her head and the last words the woman said to her, "This is all going to work out."

A few hours later, after drinking two cups of coffee and nibbling on some buttered toast from room service, she was starting to feel a little better. Sitting at the work desk with her laptop open, she started looking up what was popular in this area. Most of the attractions were seasonal. She wanted something year-round, bringing in a steady income to all the businesses. But before she could proceed, the town needed some serious sprucing up. It was looking tired and shabby. People had neglected to keep their shops looking clean. There was peeling paint on walls and dead flowers in planters. There were overflowing trash cans. What happened to the garbage pick-up? Was this all a matter of being afraid to invest in their business when no money was coming in? *It's a catch 22,* she thought. *How can they think of spending money when they don't know if there will be any more in the future?*

Taking out her sharpie, she jotted some notes down on her pad.

Number one, where is the money coming from to do the renovations? How much is needed to clean up the town? Are there low-cost options available? This was a new tactic for her to explore. She'd never dealt with clients with restrictive budgets before. The normal procedure involved lots of money being thrown at her to fix what needed fixing. Not this time.

Maybe Brian had some ideas about funding. She called down to the front desk and asked to be transferred to Brian's phone. He answered on the first ring.

"Feeling better, Anna?" he asked.

"How did you know… of course, caller ID. I am feeling better, thank you. Do you have time for a quick chat about some of the things I am considering?"

"Do you feel up to having a light lunch, say around 12:30?"

"Yes, thanks. Where should I meet you?"

"There is dining on the terrace. I think the fresh air would be good for you, and it is more private than eating inside."

"Ok, see you then." Anna was happy to do something constructive. She was not the type of person who allowed herself any downtime, sick or not. It was 11 am. She had time for a little more research before she met him.

At 12:15, Anna was dressed in slacks, soft boots, a navy cashmere sweater, and a lightweight leather jacket. She kept her hair tied at the nape of her neck with a few loose tendrils framing her face, added a dab of lipstick and a quick sweep of mascara. Gathering her notes and her briefcase, she was ready.

Always punctual, Anna walked out onto the hotel terrace at 12:30 on the dot. It overlooked the mountains, filled with the warmth of fall sunshine and a light breeze. The patio was constructed of natural stone with iron railings and glass panels to protect diners from the wind. There were a dozen round glass-topped tables spaced far enough apart to ensure privacy, but it didn't matter when there was only one other couple seated for lunch. She knew by the lack of diners Brian was also feeling the economic downturn happening in Opal Springs. The hostess walked over and welcomed her, then led her to a table closest to the railing.

Mr. Gardner will be with you shortly," she said. "May I get you something to drink?"

"Thank you, tea, please. Do you have Lapsang Souchong?"

"Yes, we do. Would you like lemon?"

"Plain is fine, thank you." Anna loved the dark smoky flavor of the tea, which contained half the caffeine of coffee. As if she was going to start worrying about caffeine now. Ha!

Anna relaxed into the comfortable padded chair and stared out into space, gathering her thoughts.

"Ms. Cartwright, the unexpected guest," said someone behind her. The tone was loud and impertinent.

Startled, it took Anna a moment to recognize the voice. Turning, she looked up into the deep brown eyes of Mayor Jared Kane. He was dressed in a casual tweed jacket, a white shirt, and pleated gray slacks.

Someone should tell him pleats make him look shorter, thought Anna, laughing to herself. She also noticed the elevated heels on his boots, the same as what he wore last night at the meeting. *Is it just me, or the shorter the politician, the higher his boot heels? Women don't do that, do they?* Then she remembered that she also used her high heels to create a persona that was larger than life. That gave her something to think about, how she manipulated people in her own Anna Cartwright way.

"Mayor Kane, to what do I owe the unexpected pleasure of seeing you here today?" She enhanced the 'unexpected.' "I thought I might be persona non gratis after last night's meeting."

"Don't be silly. Everyone is welcome in Opal Springs. I just wanted to stop by and get a proper introduction to the beautiful Ms. Cartwright. I wanted to meet you in person if we are going to work together. The hostess told me you would be dining with my old friend Brian on the terrace." He stuck out his hand for the official Mayor Kane Handshake.

Anna kept from wincing as she felt his grip. It was firm, just shy of painful, but a reminder of who was supposed to be in charge. There was always one in every crowd, or company, who felt that they could steamroll her by their handshake, their bragging about who they know and how she was just a little lady who should step back and let the man handle the situation. Even some women had learned the art of intimidation and truth be told, she half admired them. But another part of her just wanted an open and honest discussion of the facts without resorting to coercion. That's what she really wanted from this exchange. *Don't let him win, don't let it show. I know I can do this and he is not going to tell me I can't.*

"You couldn't have picked a better time; here is Brian now." Anna pulled her hand free and waggled her fingers at Brian as he came out onto the patio. The look on his face told Anna he was not pleased to see who had shown up for lunch.

Swiveling around, Mayor Kane smiled his official Mayor smile, lots of teeth and intense brown eyes glinting with superiority.

"My old friend, Brian, how lovely to see you again. I had a feeling you would want to share the delightful Ms. Cartwright with me today to go over some of her ideas."

"Did you, now?" Brian asked

Anna watched Brian skillfully hiding his irritation as well as choosing his battles. It was better to give in to this small interruption and save the big battle for later.

Brian waved for the hostess to set up another lunch setting.

"Don't bother, I don't want to interrupt your little luncheon," the Mayor said. "What I stopped by for was to invite Ms. Cartwright to dinner so we can discuss what she has in mind." Looking at Anna, he said without waiting for her to respond. "I will pick you up at 7 pm."

"Nice to see you, Brian. Until tonight, Ms. Cartwright," he said as he reached for her hand to kiss it. Yanking her hand away before he could touch her, Anna retorted. "A bit presumptuous, don't you think, Mayor Kane. "Careful of those fancy high-heeled boots. Don't trip on the way out."

He frowned as he turned and walked into the hotel.

Chapter 8

THE DINNER DATE

THE DINNER DATE

"So, Brian, what do you think he has in mind? I feel a bit like I am about to be hijacked, and my first thought is he'll try to adopt me into his campaign."

"I think you've read him just about right. He's not above taking advantage of whoever gets in his way." Brian laughed. "And you grabbed his attention last night. I'm sure you saw the look on his face. I don't think I've ever seen him lose his cool in front of his constituency before. You astonished him without ever saying a direct word to him."

"I hope I didn't cause any bad feelings. I was under the impression you were friends. Today, it feels more like adversaries." Anna asked because she didn't want to step in the middle of a small-town tussle.

"When I first moved to Opal Springs and started rebuilding the hotel, Mayor Jared, was all for it and let it be known around town, that it was because of him I was here, creating the new hotel. I didn't bother to tell people anything different because it's good to stay out of politics, if possible."

"Smart man, those are my sentiments, too," said Anna. "I've run into similar situations with large companies. There are almost always, competing interests and it was up to me to merge the conflicts into one solution that works for everyone. And make each side feel like they've won."

"Well, if I have any words of wisdom to impart, listen as much to what he isn't saying as to what he is. He's not a fool and has been running things around here for quite a long time. If he thinks the town is on your side, he will try and make it seem like it was all his idea. Bottom line, we need him to put his stamp of approval on what we do going forward." Brian raised his hand and waved the waitress over to take their order.

*****

Around 6 that evening, Anna dressed in what she considered country chic for her dinner with the Mayor. She chose skinny black leather jeans, a white silk shirt, and a tan suede bolero-style jacket. She slipped her feet into high-heeled red suede pumps and piled her hair on top of her head with wispy curls floating down in front of her ears. This would make her at least 3 inches taller than Mayor Kane. She also had advantages she wasn't afraid to use.

Anna was waiting in the lobby at 7 pm for Mayor Kane to pick her up for the "dinner date."

"Ms. Cartwright, how stunning you look tonight," said Mayor Kane as he walked into the main reception area.

"Call me Anna if I may call you Jared?" Anna reached out her hand, this time for an official handshake. Tonight, was all about business, and she was dressed in her 'take no prisoners' attire.

Mayor Kane smiled, looking up into her blue eyes.

Anna noticed that he didn't seem to mind she was taller than him by several inches. In fact, he confirmed her experience with men of this stature. He was a Napoleon type. And she was his Josephine. She awarded him a point for his belief in his own superiority despite his high-heeled cowboy boots.

Jared, aka Mayor Kane, drove to a sprawling steakhouse on the edge of town. Even though it was a Friday night, the parking lot was half full.

They parked near the front door and walked into the foyer. Mayor Kane shook hands with everyone he met and introduced Anna as 'his' special consultant for the town. She saw the knowing looks and smiled. He was a bad boy showing her off as his prize. He made it seem that she might be more than a business associate. She would have to be careful with this one, but she could tell he was already underestimating her. Silly man.

Dinner went better than Anna expected. After they were served their drinks and ordered, Jared calmed down and focused on his agenda, trying to convince Anna his plan for the resort was the way to go. He started throwing statistics and numbers at her like she was an amateur, trying to impress her with his knowledge of what works best for small towns. After all, he was the mayor of a small town and told her it would soon to be a world-famous destination. Anna felt that was stretching it, but she kept her opinions to herself.

Anna gave him her full attention, but something struck her as off about his proposal. What was he not telling her? The numbers didn't add up. And, at no time did he mention what the people thought of this plan. He talked about the townspeople like they were sheep who needed to be led around by the nose. Anna knew better. She'd heard them speak at the meeting; she'd talked to them in their shops. She was not so big-city that she thought country people were ignorant. Quite the contrary. They were sharper than a lot of her neighbors in Manhattan. They had more to lose, their livelihoods and their history.

Diverging from numbers and revenue, Jared paused and looked at her. "I have to say how impressed I was with your presentation, as short as it was, at the meeting last night. You had the crowd eating out of your hand. We will make a great team. With you upfront, the resort is a done deal."

"You present a compelling argument," Anna lied, ignoring his offer. "I am not quite ready to support this project until I check out this resort corporation. I want to know which company it is, and what their reputation is. How well do they treat their employees? How careful are they of local environments? What happens five years down the line after this resort company moves in? Does it still work?"

Jared sat back in his chair. "You should let me worry about the details. You'll have enough on your plate convincing everyone in town to sign on the dotted line. I don't think you know enough about it to handle the final transaction."

It was like waving a red flag in front of a bull. There were those words again...*I don't think you know enough, or I don't think you can...* Anna took a deep breath and remembered what was at stake. This was not the time to lose her temper. She knew she could do whatever she set her mind on.

"Jared, there is a lot we'd have to agree on before I would ever recommend a plan I haven't vetted. Do you think you could send over the information I've requested in the morning? I need to see the fine print." Anna beamed. "I would love a cup of Frappuccino."

*****

The return ride to the hotel was quiet. Jared didn't say a word. Anna was also thinking about how to keep him from imploding when she turned down his proposal. He wasn't paying her bill, but she wanted to keep him on her side as much as possible. Life can be complicated.

Chapter 9

DEAL WITH THE DEVIL

Anna was not surprised Mayor Jared did not deliver the information she'd requested about the resort. She continued to see him around town, but he nodded and hurried on his way, afraid to look her in the eye. She could only guess at what machinations he was working on, but he was leaving her alone for the time being.

Over the next couple of weeks, Anna spent a lot of time getting to know many of the people in town. She held impromptu meetings at the diner, invited individuals to the hotel for lunch or coffee, she stopped by the local high school to meet with the principal and some of the teachers. She wanted their direct input. What did they think the problem was? Did they have any thoughts about how they wanted to see the town change? And she took abundant notes. Though this one-on-one interaction was not how she usually worked, she found that she enjoyed it. The people were getting to know her. She sensed that they trusted her. They seemed to recognize it was also to her advantage to make them all successful.

Anna spent most evenings with Brian, not always for dinner, sometimes just for coffee or a glass of wine to go over her expanding notebook of ideas. She enjoyed his quick wit and his passion for this little town in the mountains. She tried not to think of him as anything but a client, but it was getting harder and harder to do. He was tall, his rugged physical presence oozing sex appeal, and his deep green eyes and black hair curling over his ears captivated her. He was one of the most intriguing men she'd ever met. She knew so little about him, except that he'd lived in some exotic locales and trained at some of the best hospitality schools in Europe. And he never stepped over the line with her, always respectful and impersonal enough to be frustrating. She sometimes wished the…*Stop it, Anna, you don't have time for anything but business.* She sighed.

A day later, Anna met Brian for breakfast on the terrace. The weather was still unseasonably warm, turning into a long slow fall which was unusual in the San Juan mountains. There was a tension in the air making it feel like the town was holding its breath, keeping the snow away until just the right moment. And there were so few outsiders visiting that their passing didn't even stir the leaves on the sidewalks.

"Brian, I have the beginnings of a plan. I need your response because I want to get this underway before the snow starts." Anna sipped her creamy coffee and nibbled on a croissant.

Brian smiled. "Let's hear it. Just so you know, I have also been talking to everyone. They think you are going to pull a rabbit out of the hat for them."

"No pressure," she laughed as she opened her notebook and pulled out a lengthy handwritten list of names and items next to them. "I read an article about sprucing up towns anyone could have found. It just takes someone willing to start the process. Everyone will feel better seeing signs and front doors with fresh paint, streets and sidewalks patched, windows washed, and planters filled with fall herbage. Since money is in such short supply, I have been asking everyone what they have in storage, unused cans of paint, half-used bags of concrete, cleaning supplies for windows. Here is a list of who has what and is willing to donate to the community."

Brian looked over the lengthy list. "I am impressed with the number of names and supplies you got people to donate to the cause."

"I know this is not the full answer to the problems here, but we have to start somewhere, and anything that brings some pride back into the town will have a positive effect for the next stage of the plan." Anna still didn't know what it would be, but she sure hoped it would hit her like a bolt of lightning rather than a bucket of cold water. It was unusual for her not to have all the answers lined up and ready to go this late in the game, but she had never attempted something like this before.

"Have you considered grants?" Brian asked.

"Grants were the first things I thought of but dismissed after seeing the problems inherent in getting one in time to do any good in the immediate future. Grants take anywhere from six months to a year to be approved, and that is after they have been submitted within specific guidelines, which requires an expert grant writer, and then you must beat out thousands of others requesting the same grant money. Opal Springs doesn't have time to wait for all of that to happen. And it wouldn't be a sure thing." Anna took a deep breath.

"I also spoke with the high school principal, and she is willing to give the juniors and seniors a couple of days off to help with the various jobs. We need to clean-up, paint, wash windows, and clear the fountain. We are going to start with an old-fashioned clean-out and clean-up day."

"I can offer an incentive prize. Kids are good at volunteering but better when they see something at the end making it more fun and something to work for." Brian jotted down a few notes.

"Thank you, Brian. It will all help." Anna continued, "I am not sure how I am going to get him to agree, but I need the Mayor to hold a town meeting in the park in two days to announce the Opal Springs Spruce Up Day."

Brian smiled at her, eyes twinkling, "You'll think of something. You've got his number."

Anna thought for a moment, a sly smiled shifting across her face. "I know how to get him to agree. A little subterfuge goes a long way for a good cause, don't you think?"

Brian laughed out loud.

*****

"Jared, we haven't spoken in a couple of weeks. I have been thinking about your proposal. Would you like to meet me for coffee?" Anna used her best business voice with a bit of cream in the inflection.

"Anna, funny you should call. I would be delighted. I have a better idea. Come to my office, and I will have coffee and brunch items to nibble on. Say tomorrow at 10 am?" After he ended the call, Mayor Jared smiled and thought. *So, Ms. Cartwright, did you come to your senses? You finally realized you need me after all.*

*****

At 10 am, Anna met the Mayor at his office with her briefcase and her iPad. She was dressed down for this meeting, wearing flat shoes, jeans, and a silky blue shirt which emphasized the icy blue of her eyes. She needed Jared on her side to make this work. This was her 'put him at ease' wardrobe.

The office was large enough to accommodate a sofa and coffee table along with the desk and filing cabinets. The coffee table was laid out with a carafe of coffee, cream in a china pot, and a dish of sugar cubes. A white china plate held a mouth-watering assortment of miniature scones, muffins, and blueberry tarts.

"Thank you for seeing me." Anna held out her hand to shake.

"My pleasure, Anna. Sit down and have some coffee and a pastry." He indicated the sofa. When they were both seated and had taken a sip of coffee, he continued. "What can I do for you?"

"I know you must be very busy working on the resort project." Anna looked at him, not reminding him he neglected to send over the materials she asked for at their previous encounter. "But I need a favor, and I'm sure it will help with your project or should I say, 'our project' as well."

Anna watched him drop his guard as he settled on the settee, sipping his coffee. She had seen his type before and knew he was envisioning buckets of money coming his way.

"I was sure you would agree with me, and this could be very lucrative for both of us. What do you have in mind?" Mayor Kane asked her with a smirk.

Anna was a little taken off guard. What did he mean by very lucrative for him and for her if she went along with him? "I'm not sure I understand. What do you, I mean 'we' stand to gain from this?"

"I want to make sure we are a team on this. Are we a team, Anna?" He looked directly at her without blinking.

"I am here for Opal Springs, and since you are a big part of the town, I am onboard. Now, what precisely are you talking about?" Anna smiled in her best conspiratorial fashion, hoping she wouldn't regret cozying up to this sleazy little mayor.

For the next twenty minutes, Jared Kane, the illustrious Mayor of Opal Springs, proceeded to fill her in on his back-dealings with a resort company called Live & Renew Resort. He told her he owned a large piece of property just outside of town which was considered part of a wildlife protection area, but he knew someone who could delist it and allow him to sell to the resort with the right payoff. Once the resort started building there, it would be easy to convince the townspeople to sell their businesses. Once the contracts were signed, half of them would be demolished to make way for bars and hot tub facilities, and other businesses. Anna cringed. This guy was worse than she had imagined. He would turn Opal Springs into the kind of trashy seashore town she'd seen when a new business moved in promising wealth to the locals. The resort would make money, but the rest of the town would be at their mercy and reap only the headaches.

"And what do you need to make this happen?" she asked, afraid she already knew the answer.

"I need you, darling. The people here like you, believe in you. Whatever you say, they will go along with. And I guarantee I will share some of the proceeds with you. Who doesn't like a big wad of cash showing up in their checking account?" Mayor Kane winked at her as he said this.

Oh my God, he is really trying to buy me and screw the town. This is going to be a challenge keeping control of the situation. Anna took a deep breath. "Here is my first suggestion. To cheer up the people here, put them in a good mood, I am proposing a special day to clean up the town: paint, plant, repair, and anything else to lift the people's spirits." She pulled out her list of names and contributors of supplies for the event. "And what I would like you to do is to call a town meeting in the central square and announce the Spruce-Up-Day. They will feel better knowing you're on board and..." Anna winced. "Have their best interests at heart."

Chapter 10
THE BIG SPRUCE-UP

THE BIG SPRUCE-UP

Mayor Kane started out the town meeting by walking through the crowd and shaking hands with some of the locals before stepping up on the platform, like a prize fighter getting into the ring. He smiled at all the attention, but everyone knew he was a bit of a crowd hog. The Mayor did his thing, talking about his love for the town and how it was all going to change for the better.

There was very little enthusiasm from the crowd on the Mayor's usual platitudes. Then he introduced Anna and the people moved a little closer to the stage.

"Thank you all for coming today." Anna beamed. "I am so excited to tell you the first stage of the plan, that's Plan with a capital P."

There was very little response from the people gathered around. They had no idea what she was talking about and weren't going to agree to anything until they heard the details.

"So, what's this big plan that's going to save our cabooses here?" said Freddie from the belts and boot shop.

Anna was so confident in this first stage that she didn't stop to think how it really sounded to desperate people.

"I'm introducing the Big Spruce-up Day. We are going to clean up and paint the town and clear out the rubbish and make this place look like a wonderful family friendly town to visit again."

"How is painting going to bring the town back? We're just putting lipstick on a pig," said Frank from the Barbecue restaurant.

"How much is this going to cost?" shouted out another voice. "I don't have an extra dime to waste on fancy paint jobs."

"How long will my business be closed?"

"Do we need permits?"

Anna raised her hand in the air. Quiet descended on the crowd. "Forgive me for not sharing the details with you and assuming you would just go along with the plan. That was a bit presumptuous on my part. This is how I've envisioned doing this, but I need you to hear me out before you make a decision. Agreed?"

Lots of heads nodded yes and an old fellow called out, "Give us the details pretty lady."

Over the next hour Anna proceeded to outline what she had in mind. Most of the materials were already sitting unused in people's back rooms and garages and sheds. It wouldn't cost much. Permits were not needed for painting doors and window frames. Sweeping sidewalks was free and cleaning out flower beds and planting some winter greenery donated by the nursery just took some manpower. At the end of the day, she had them on her side. It wasn't more than they could do, and it would make the town feel fresher, like the people who lived here cared.

"I've said enough. When someone tells me I can't, when I know I can, it's like waving a red flag. We can make this work together and it is only the beginning. Are you with me?"

Everyone started chattering, talking about what they could do and how nice it would be to see the town freshened up a bit. Like Anna said. This was only Part 1 of her bigger plan to follow.

"Yes, we're with you roared the crowd," their eyes sparkling with real interest.

The town meeting finished as an enormous success. The Mayor had done his thing, talking up his plan and the wellbeing of everybody in the town. He swore he wanted Opal Springs and all the people to recover from the financial disaster of the last two years. Visitors would return in droves and that they would all make money and be happy ever after. But it was Anna who stole the show. Her Big Spruce-Up plan was simple enough and cheap enough that everyone could envision themselves as a part of it.

At the end of the presentation, Brian came up to stand beside the Mayor and Anna and announced he was donating $5000 for a scholarship from his own personal funds. A drawing would choose the winner from all students who participated in the town clean-up. Loud cheers erupted from the crowd. They hadn't felt this good in a long while. What also helped was the Mayor heeded Anna's request not to mention the resort until a later date.

The Spruce-Up started the next day. Centrally located, the building where the snow trucks were stored was opened, and volunteers dropped off supplies. Sue Johnson from the Fine Scents Candle Shoppe kept track of who was dropping off and who was picking up supplies. The high school kids showed up in droves and helped carry buckets of paint, swept sidewalks, and cleaned out gutters. They made themselves useful to everyone.

Volunteers painted front doors in whatever colors were donated. It worked out better than Anna could have guessed. There were apple-red doors, sky-blue doors, forest-green doors, and even a plum-purple door. It made the main street look cheerful and fresh. People smiled seeing these new colors glow in between the regular brown and gray doors. The ladies quilting society washed windows and refreshed planter boxes with new dirt and winter plants donated from the local nursery. Some of the elf mailboxes were repainted to remind people of what this town had been.

Kirk acted as the town maintenance man as well as the Opal Springs chauffeur. He reattached sagging shutters and restored the fountain. When the water spouted into the air and refilled the circular pool around the centerpiece, the clamor was deafening. The centerpiece was masterful, a handsome stone-carved Native American chief with an eagle resting on his upraised hand.

And to keep everyone energized, Molly from The Hot Pot Diner was there, serving coffee, water, and soft drinks along with egg salad sandwiches.

Unbeknownst to anyone, Mary Jefferson sat on a stool on the second floor of the Opal Springs Library, looking through the antique telescope focused on the town square. She watched the energy and enthusiasm of her neighbors and friends, created in large part by the lovely, red-headed stranger in town. A glowing orb floated behind her. "Tahoma, I had a feeling she was the one." Mary smiled, climbed off her stool, realigned the telescope, and headed down the stairs to the front desk. There was a cup of hot tea waiting on the counter.

"This was a great day, Anna. You reined in our illustrious Mayor. How did you manage that slippery politician?" Brian looked tired and happy as he sipped a glass of wine at the hotel bar. He'd contributed a lot of physical labor as well as suggestions for color schemes to the owners of the various businesses.

At first Anna laughed, then she grimaced. "If I may be blunt, the Mayor is not honest. You mentioned before in passing he had ulterior motives. Well, by my agreeing to go along with him, he told me everything, maybe not everything, but enough to know where his true interests lie." Anna exhaled. "And the town is not at the top of his list."

"I was hoping my information was faulty on that front. Did he happen to mention anyone connected with the wildlife protection agency?

"So, you knew what he was planning all along? Why didn't you say anything?"

"I received a call a couple of months ago from someone I know at the wildlife center. This guy thought I should know someone from Opal Springs attempted to bribe him to delist some property belonging to a certain local Mayor." he paused. "You have just confirmed my worst fears." Brian looked crestfallen. "I thought he was a friend. How could he sink so low? But my acquaintance at the wildlife center assured me he wouldn't go along with the plan. It might even be criminal to offer a bribe. For the time being, he agreed to play along to see how far our illustrious Mayor would go."

Anna thought for a moment, toying with her still full wine glass. "That's excellent news. It means Jared has no chance of selling his protected property to anyone, let alone this resort company. But it also means I still have to pull the rabbit out of the hat." She drank her whole glass down, not even tasting it.

Chapter 11

THE REAL OPAL SPRINGS

THE REAL OPAL SPRINGS

nna woke around 7 am, still tired but satisfied she had at last accomplished something. It wasn't much, but it was a start. She dressed and walked downstairs, heading for the terrace and her usual start to the day, coffee. Sipping it, she savored the aroma as well as the taste. *How do they make their coffee taste so good?* she wondered anew. *The beans contribute to the aroma, but what gives it such a unique taste?* She would have to ask Brian.

"Good morning Ms. Cartwright," said Brian looking far more cheerful than he was last night. "Are you up for a little adventure, a break from Opal Springs, the town?"

Anna thought about it. "Sounds good to me, I need to refresh my batteries. What do you have in mind?"

"It's a surprise. Do you have hiking boots?" he asked, looking down at her loafers.

"No, but I know where to get some. And it'll make one of the shop keepers happy to have a customer."

"Meet me here in an hour, and we'll take the day off. I need a break myself."

*****

An hour later, Anna was standing in the lobby sporting new hiking boots and extra thick socks to keep from getting blisters. She was wearing jeans, a long-sleeved shirt, a parka with a hood, and had her hair tied with a leather thong. Brian met her, dressed in jeans, boots, and a heavy cable knit sweater. Anna couldn't help drawing in a breath. *Whoa, what a hunk*, thought Anna. *It'll be nice to interact with him without all the hoopla and drama going on around here.*

"Here is a small rucksack for your phone, water bottle and sunscreen if you need it." Brian handed her a lightweight backpack emblazoned with the Opal Springs Hotel logo on the front. "The 4-wheel drive is behind the hotel. Ready to go?"

"Lead me on."

Half an hour later, after driving through the thick forest up a steep dirt incline, they reached the end of the road. Brian pulled into the small parking area. Anna was relieved to find no one in sight, no cars, and no other hikers. After Brian turned the jeep off, all Anna could hear were the clicking of the engine as it cooled and the high-pitched calls of eagles circling in the sky above them. They got out of the vehicle and breathed in the fresh mountain air.

"This is beautiful," murmured Anna looking around. "Do you come here often?"

"Every chance I get. This is the best place I've found to get out of my own way when I am working on a problem. I thought you might find it helpful."

Brian reached for his backpack, twice the size of Anna's and pulled it over his shoulders. He then helped Anna slip the smaller one over her shoulders.

"Ready? It's not far, about a mile. It should take us a little less than an hour. The elevation gain is around 300 feet, but it's rocky, and there are a couple of streams to ford. Have you done much hiking?"

"I have done quite a bit of cross-country skiing and hiked up a couple of mountains in Europe, but nothing in the last six months. I hope I haven't lost my strength."

"As simple as this looks, it's not recommended for inexperienced hikers. It requires some complicated navigating around overgrown and hidden trails and water crossings with tricky footing." Brian looked at her in her hiking gear. "I don't think you will have any problems. It's not like you're a total couch potato." He laughed when she smirked at him.

Brian walked into the woods on the little-used trail indicating Anna should follow. The path was so rocky she spent more time watching her feet to keep from twisting an ankle or falling over rocks in the small streams, than watching where she was going.

"Oof! Oh, sorry," said Anna as she walked straight into the rear of Brian.

"Trust your feet and keep your eyes up. You don't want to poke yourself in the eye with one of those Blue Spruce branches. It might be dangerous as well as painful."

A bit embarrassed, Anna nodded. The smell of pine needles from the tall Ponderosa Pines filled her nose with a light spearmint aroma. The shorter blue spruce seemed to prefer growing closer to the streams and their branches were full of spiky needles. Brian held up his hand, signaling a stop. "Do you hear something?"

Anna stopped and listened. A low roar vibrated through the trees in front of them. "Is that a river?"

"Wait and see. It's not much further. You go first. We're almost there."

Anna walked around him and entered the end of a narrow canyon. Here the sound was overwhelming. Her chest vibrated with an unseen power. She could feel the fine droplets in the air before she saw the source.

She walked a dozen more steps until she rounded a corner in the chasm. The scene exploded across all her senses. At the end of the narrow gorge, cascading sheets of water plummeted down the cliff face, tumbling over boulders at the bottom and into the river. The roar was now so loud her ears thrummed from the pressure. The mist from the falls filled the canyon and covered her face with cool droplets. Soon, her hair was dripping. Anna felt like she was plunging into another world light years away from her everyday experience. Brian reached out and carefully took her hand and squeezed it. He, too, seemed to be mesmerized by the power of the falls. They stood together, blinking the water from their eyes. Anna was too astonished to say anything.

Anna didn't have an inkling how long they stood under the roaring water's spell. She thought she saw sparkles of light racing up and down the length of the fall of water but dismissed it as an illusion from the sun striking the moisture in the air.

"Time for the rest of the surprise," Brian said as he turned Anna around with a gentle push on her shoulder and guided her from the roar of the water into a small opening in the canyon wall. The sound of the falls became muted enough to talk again. Anna shook the water out of her hair.

"I have never seen anything so unexpected in all of my travels. This place is gorgeous and mysterious." Her eyes were sparkling with an inner joy she couldn't quite define. She felt an unusual energy all around her, causing her skin to vibrate. Her vision was sharper, her hearing tuned into the sound of the water falling and the sound of birds calling to each other. She looked up and saw what she guessed to be the same two eagles. A shiver ran down her spine, like a finger had run down her back with the lightest of touches. She felt like she knew this place, like a déjà vu just happened.

"This is where the real Opal Springs starts, Anna. Few people take the time to come up here and see this wonder. Thank goodness. The waterfall doesn't have a name you will find on any map. The Native Americans call it *The Water that Thunders*, and the runoff fills the springs leading to the town. Even if you know where it is, people will take the easier path and pass this one by."

"But why is it called Opal Springs? I haven't heard of opals being common in this part of the country."

Brian chuckled. "Most people think it is called Opal Springs because of the opalescent shine on the rocks in the springs closer to town. But this is one of my favorite secrets that I will share with you. A rare pocket of ironstone sediment thousands of years old, was discovered by a local tribe. Silica from dissolved sand trickled down cracks and crevices and formed a unique type of opal called the boulder opal. Generally, the opal is found within boulders which need to be broken open. The colors are glorious. I have one back at the lodge that I will show you. If people knew this was where it was discovered, this place would soon be trashed by treasure hunters digging up the ground and destroying the environment. I am trusting you to keep it a secret."

"Thank you for sharing and for bringing me here." Anna found it hard to say anything, for what could she say that could describe her feelings?

"Are you hungry?" Brian reached behind and unbuckled his backpack. Inside was a tiny camp stove, coffee pot, and containers of fresh-ground coffee and cream. He unwrapped two chicken salad sandwiches on fresh-baked baguettes and laid them out on two metal camping plates.

"You are quite the Boy Scout. Always prepared." Anna teased.

"I just have to fill the pot with water from the waterfall. If you think the coffee in town is good, wait 'til you taste this made fresh from the source."

He returned about five minutes later with the coffee pot and water bottles filled with water from the falls. Anna took a sip. "Brian, this water tastes almost minty. It's delicious."

"I think it's from the pine tree resin in the air. I have never tasted water like this anyplace else I have ever been. It's a well-kept secret with those who have been brave enough to make the trek here."

Brian set up the tiny camp stove and set the coffee brewing. Soon, the aroma was almost more than Anna could bear. "Is it ready yet? I'm salivating."

Brian poured her a cup as she made herself comfortable on the blanket he pulled out of his backpack. The first taste of the coffee was almost electrifying. "Ohh, my. This is even better than the coffee in town. What is going on here?"

Brian laughed. "I knew you would appreciate it. The main source of water for the town of Opal Springs comes from the real Opal Springs as it permeates the aquifer in the area. It is full of minerals: iron, zinc, copper, iodine, calcium, phosphorus, magnesium, and a bunch of others. I've had it tested."

"You could bottle this water, you could...." Anna stopped. "You could bottle this water, make the Opal Springs brand."

Brian thought about it with a slight frown. "I have considered it, but something stops me. Did you notice anything unusual about the falls?"

"I thought I was seeing things, but I swear I saw bright lights racing up and down the falls. Did you see them, too?"

"Some of the old-timers swear the falls are haunted by the Native tribes who used to live and hunt on this land. The falls were where they came to talk to the thunder spirits. I think it's why so few people can find the falls. To me, they feel protected. I believe those who pass some kind of test are the special people allowed to see them."

"Do you mean I passed the test? It has to be because I'm with you." Anna felt a ripple of energy run down her spine. This was a new Brian she hadn't noticed before. He was in his element here in the woods.

"Forgive me if I am being too personal, but do you have Native American blood in your ancestry?"

Brian smiled. "Maybe I'll tell you when I get to know you better."

He said when, not if. Anna smiled to herself. She thought she understood why he didn't want to advertise this water, this place. It was sacred to him. She thought about the word sacred. She couldn't remember ever having thought anything was sacred before, but it felt right to describe this place as sacred.

*****

After lunch, they began talking about the local environment. Brian told her about a hot spring he found underneath the old foundation of a shed behind the original hotel. He wanted to make it a feature, an outdoor heated soaking pool but hadn't gotten around to it yet. There were also rumors of other hot springs close to the town, filled with the minerals from the underground aquifer which made the water and the coffee taste so good.

"Soaking in mineral hot springs is a natural way to detoxify and a gentle remedy for skin ailments like acne, eczema, and psoriasis. It also helps to soothe joint pain," Brian said.

This was starting to sound like a plan to Anna. A new type of calling card for Opal Springs. Maybe the resort concept was not so far-fetched, but not like what Mayor Jared Kane was planning. She was beginning to realize that the town already held the key to its own success without selling out to anyone. A whole new group of visitors would stand in line to come and visit once they heard what Opal Springs was able to offer. Anna started to feel like she was on solid ground. She knew how to work with this. It wasn't her usual brainstorm, but it was just as powerful as a deeply flowing river, and it filled her with a secret satisfaction none of the other jobs had given her in the past.

They discussed how to implement her new ideas until late in the afternoon. "We'd better start getting ready to go before it gets dark. This trail is tricky enough in the daytime," said Brian. "But let's take one more look at the falls before we leave."

Streaks of yellow light filtered through the tall trees and tinted the froth of the water as it hit the rocks, a silky pink and gold. Anna saw the sparkling lights coming down the falls again. She smiled before she turned and started walking with Brian down the trail to the jeep.

Chapter 12

THE PLAN

THE PLAN

Anna went to the town center the next day and stood on the first steps leading up to the fountain, and announced she was calling a town meeting to take place later in the afternoon, around 5 pm. She printed out simple flyers at the hotel copy center, which she passed out to everyone who walked by. Although there weren't many people, the word soon got out. The flyer said Anna had some important news to share, listing the time and the place. This time, she felt secure enough to call a meeting without Mayor Jared's help. It was exhilarating to experience the people's response to her.

The excitement began to build. Everyone was waiting for this. They trusted Anna and knew she cared about them. Besides, old Mary Jefferson from the library intimated Anna might have been sent to them by the old ones. And no one ever disputed Mary Jefferson. She had never been known to be wrong, and that was a long time to think about.

By 5 pm, the town square was filled.

Standing on the top step of the fountain surround, Anna looked ready to take on the world. She was dressed in black and white—black trousers and a white jacket with a soft pale gray blouse. She was also wearing her power shoes, four-inch red suede heels.

"Thank you for coming." She looked around the crowd and clasped her hands in gratitude. "First, I want to thank everyone who turned out for the Spruce-Up-Day. Your town looks glorious, fresh and clean, and ready for business."

"Damn right," shouted Frank from the barbecue restaurant.

"Woohoo!" whooped a bunch of ladies from the Opal Springs quilting society.

Others nodded their heads and clapped in agreement.

"Second, Brian Gardner has an announcement to make before I begin. Brian, come on up."

Brian walked up to stand beside Anna. He was carrying a large glass jar with folded slips of paper inside. Even in her high heels, he stood three or four inches taller.

"Lord, don't they look nice together," whispered Sue Johnson from the candle shop. A couple of the ladies next to her wagged their heads in agreement, drooling over the handsome Brian Gardner as well as Anna's red shoes.

"I have the names of all of the high school students who helped with the clean-up. Are you ready to find out who is the winner of the $5000 scholarship?"

Loud cheering erupted from everyone in the town square.

"Molly Wilson, will you do the honors?" Brian extended his hand to encourage everyone's favorite waitress from the Hot Pot Diner, to come forward.

"Oh my," Molly said in her rough voice. "I would be delighted."

Still wearing her coffee-stained apron, Molly walked up the steps and stood next to Brian.

"Whenever you're ready, just reach in and pull out a name."

Molly, blushing with embarrassment and pride, reached in, and pulled out a slip of paper. Unfolding it, she read out the name. "Whitney Ann Morris."

A teenager from the middle of the crowd screamed in shock and joy as she ran up to the front. "That's me. I won! I won!"

"Congratulations, Whitney Ann Morris," Brian said as he shook her hand. "Come by the hotel tomorrow, and I will make sure your scholarship is applied to the school of your choice."

"Thank you, Brian, for the generous contribution. You may have just changed the future for this young lady." Anna smiled at Brian and turned to the crowd.

"I have recently come into some important information about your beautiful town which could be the saving grace without selling out your birthright. I will need all of you to get on board. It will take a little bit of hard work, but I have seen all of you are more than capable and ready to roll up your sleeves."

Anna looked at Brian to see how she was doing. He grinned at her, his green eyes twinkling. "You've got this," he mouthed.

"I have discovered a secret a lot of you have been keeping just for yourselves. I don't blame you, but I think now is the time to ask yourself. What is more important, your own secret mineral bath or something that will benefit lots of people with aches and pains and help fill up your bank accounts and save your town?"

There was a stunned silence. Everyone knew what she was talking about. They never considered before it might be a good idea to share what they'd all been enjoying for generations.

"You have always been known as the Christmas town with spirit, but you haven't been sharing what was most important. Your town can help heal people."

A deep sigh of realization wafted over the crowd, like a long-dormant flower starting to bloom.

"Let's hear the plan," called out Freddie Lopez. A chorus of other voices joined in.